NEIGHBOURHOOD WITCH

MARY HOOPER

WALKER BOOKS

AND SUBSIDIARIES

LONDON • BOSTON • SYDNEY • AUCKLAND

First published 2004 by Walker Books Ltd
87 Vauxhall Walk, London SE11 5HJ

2 4 6 8 10 9 7 5 3 1

Text © 2004 Mary Hooper
Cover/title page illustration © 2004 David Roberts

This book has been typeset in Sabon

Printed in Great Britain by J.H. Haynes & Co. Ltd

British Library Cataloguing in Publication Data:
a catalogue record for this book is
available from the British Library

ISBN 0-7445-8360-8

www.walkerbooks.co.uk

You may have seen a bright yellow sign somewhere near where you live which says: NEIGHBOURHOOD WATCH. But look again – not *all* of them say this.

Some of them actually say:

NEIGHBOURHOOD WITCH

If you see a sign like this, don't tell *anyone*! If people find out there's a witch living nearby, they might panic and run round in circles and start tearing their hair out. (And sometimes the witch's hair as well.)

This is the story of one neighbourhood witch and her daughter, Amber.

NEIGHBOURHOOD 1 WITCH

"**M**um!" I said, staring at her, horrified. "You're not coming up to the school looking like that!"

"Why not?" she said, and twirled around so that her black cloak opened out like bats' wings. She lifted her tall, pointy hat. "What's the matter, Amber? Don't you want anyone to know I'm a witch?"

I gave a short scream and she cackled with laughter. "Only joking! Of course I'm not going dressed in my ceremonial gear. I just thought I'd cheer you up a bit. You've got a face longer than a broomstick."

"Yeah, well, thanks a bundle, Mum," I said. "Now go and change."

I sighed. I've known there was something odd about my mum ever since my third birthday when she'd pointed her fingers at a plate and magicked a cake out of thin air. She'd told me then about being a witch and I remember being distinctly unimpressed, especially as the birthday cake was actually *made* of thin air and tasted of nothing. It had no currants or sugar or nuts or eggs, it was just a pretend cake. I realized then that having a witch for a mum was going to have its drawbacks.

A moment later she came downstairs

again, dressed in black jeans and a jumper.

"Ready, my little witchette?" She smiled at me, pulling one of those faces that mums have when they're peering into prams.

"Don't call me that!" I said, scowling. "And I've been ready for *ages*."

"Got your school books?"

"They're upstairs. I'll go and get them."

"Amber," she said gently, "why don't you *magic* them down? Stand at the foot of the stairs and extend your arm and—"

"I know how to do it!"

"Well, then."

"I just don't *want* to."

This, you see, was the other big drawback to having a mum who was a witch. Magic was the family business, passed on through the generations, the same as other families pass on red hair or sticking-out ears. All my female ancestors had been witches who'd passed their skills on to their daughters, then parked their broomsticks when their powers had faded. Great-gran had been a witch, Gran had been a witch, Mum was a witch and I was a witch. Whether I liked it or not.

And I did not.

Mum shook her head sadly. "Sometimes I think you must be a changeling child swapped over by fairies. I can't understand your attitude, darling. After all:

A witch is a treasure,
a wonderful thing,
like a fish in the sea
or a bird on the wing."

"Per-lease," I said. I'd grown up with this ditty, the same as you might have grown up with "Twinkle, twinkle little star". I gave her my version of it:

> "*A witch is embarrassing,*
> *everyone knows that.*
> *Being a witch*
> *is a lot of old hat!*"

"Amber, what a terrible thing to say." She tucked her arm through mine. "It's not really that bad, is it?"

I nodded. "Yes, it is!" I said. "I just want to be ordinary."

"Ordinary!" Mum lifted her hands in horror, as if I'd said I wanted to shave my head and have nose piercings.

"Look, forget it," I said hastily. "I'm

starting a new school, no one knows us and I want to make sure it stays that way. They're not to find out that you're a witch!"

Neighbourhood witches are supposed to be a secret. They're sent to help the community, but the community isn't supposed to know they're there. This is because in olden days women were burnt at stakes just for being witches (and though I know how the people must have felt, even *I* think this is taking things too far). So those in charge – Witches International, known as the WI – keep quiet about neighbourhood witches in case people panic when they find they've got one living nearby; start worrying that they'll be overrun with black cats or turned into toads. Neighbourhood witches are *supposed* to work undercover.

At our last place, though, they'd started to suspect something. Mum, you see, is quite showy. She likes dressing up in traditional costume, enjoys nothing more than cooking a nourishing broth in the cauldron over the fire, has a habit of talking to our cat in front of people, and also keeps a couple of pet bats hanging inside her umbrella. If this wasn't enough, on Halloween she *would* insist on going into the garden to bow to the moon stark naked, even though I tried to stop her. Sure enough, someone saw her, our neighbours asked questions, there was a lot of gossip at the corner shop, and someone contrived a plan to see if Mum could walk across running water (which she couldn't, of course, being a true witch). Once the WI found out about this rumour, they moved us on quite swiftly.

This time, in *this* house, I'd made her promise that she wouldn't do anything to make anyone suspicious – wouldn't sail her broomstick too close to the wind, as the saying goes. I wanted to lead a nice, ordinary sort of life.

This meant that Mum was not to:

- mutter incantations and spells (for instance, if someone pinched her place in a supermarket queue)

- have a conversation with the cat when anyone was around

- leave the house, naked or otherwise, on Halloween

- nip down to the shops on her

broomstick or use WATER (Witches Alternative Transport – Eastern Region, i.e. instant travel) except in the most urgent circumstances

• wear witch's clothes (or only on agreed ceremonial occasions).

I'd also made her promise to concentrate on microwaved rather than boil-in-a-cauldron foods, dump the bats, have a normal hairstyle rather than long, black tangles and try to be an ordinary human mother in every way possible.

If you knew my mum, though…

To tell the truth, I didn't hold out much hope.

She lifted her arm. "It's so easy, Amber – just point your fingers and give a little wriggle and the magic will travel in a lovely, twinkly way down your arm and—"

"No!" I said firmly, and before she could magic my books downstairs I ran up and got them myself. I wasn't going to use my witchy powers! I reckoned that if I didn't actually develop them, they'd gradually die away. Things did, sometimes. I'd heard about someone who'd learned to play the piano and then not played for years, so had lost the knack. Also, someone else, me, who within six months had forgotten every word of the French that she'd picked up when her mum had sent on a Foreign Witch Exchange.

Going out of the front door I looked up at our **NEIGHBOURHOOD WITCH** sign. These are put up by the WI, are made of painted yellow metal and are exactly the same as the real NEIGHBOURHOOD WATCH signs in every way, except that if you look closely the "a" is very thin. No one ever seems to notice this, though. No one knows when a neighbourhood witch is in residence. And I wanted it to stay that way.

NEIGHBOURHOOD **2** WiTCH

"**A**re we late?" Mum asked as we started off down the road.

I looked at my watch. "Just right. Fifteen minutes to Registration."

"Are you sure you don't want to take the broomstick, Amber? It'd be much quicker. Or we could go by WATER."

I gave her a look. "No!" I said. Broomsticks being considered rather old-fashioned now, Mum sometimes used

Witches Alternative Transport to get an instant transfer from one place to another. You can imagine how embarrassing this can be (not to mention rather scary for anyone watching), suddenly to appear somewhere without a word of warning.

"Well, anyway," she said, "say goodbye to Mortimer. You know how difficult he can be if you don't wish him a nice day."

I sighed and looked over our fence. Mum's great big black cat was sitting amid the tangled grass and brambles of our garden (witches don't do pretty flowers and neat lawns) looking at me with a spiteful eye. It was depressing to think I was probably going to inherit this cat – witches' cats being everlasting. I mean, I *like* cats – nice fluffy ones and especially tortoiseshell – but Mortimer was an ugly great thing with slitty eyes and chewed ears, more tiger than tabby. Whoever said that black cats were lucky obviously hadn't seen Mortimer.

"Goodbye, Mortimer, dear..." Mum prompted me.

"G'bye," I muttered.

"Goodbye-Mortimer-have-a-pleasant-day," Mum repeated.

I said it. The cat didn't move. Didn't even blink. It's supposed to be in charge of Lost Cats but I've never seen it actually do anything useful.

"Why can't we have something better than him," I said as we walked down the road. "If we had a puppy, I could take it out on walks..."

From behind me I heard a long, low *"Grrr..."*

"You don't mean that, Amber!" Mum said hastily. "Do you, darling? You love dear Mortimer."

There was another *"Grrr..."*

"Yeah. I really love Mortimer," I said obediently, crossing my fingers. "Just love that cat."

The school was about five minutes away and the closer we got, the more I regretted letting Mum come with me. There were other kids all around us and none of them had their mums with them.

"You can go home now," I said when the school gates were in sight. "I'm not going to get lost."

"Go home?" she said. "I'm not going home on your first day at a new school. I want to meet your teacher. Get to know him. It's only polite."

"I'll send him your best wishes," I said.

"Amber, I promise I won't do anything to embarrass you," Mum said, speaking in her smarmiest and sincerest voice.

I just looked at her. She was an embarrassment just being there; she didn't have to *do* anything.

The playground was filled with girls wearing the Cheetham red and grey uniform, but I spotted a whole load about my age gathered round a low brick wall, some sitting, some slouching around beside them.

"We'll wait here on our own," I hissed at Mum, but she was already striding across the tarmac towards them. Knowing what she could do, fearing what she might say, I had no alternative but to run after her.

Mum beamed at them and said, "Hello, girls!" in a children's TV sort of voice. She turned to me, "Now, Amber, introduce yourself to your new friends!" she said, and I wanted to curl up quietly and die. This was why life was so difficult with Mum. She doesn't *do* ordinary.

Everyone turned to stare, and Mum poked me to say something.

"Hi. I'm Amber Collins," I mumbled.

A few girls murmured something back, then they all turned away to look at what they'd been looking at before, which were the trainers being worn by a tall girl with thickly gelled hair. The trainers were super-trendy with pumped-up soles, padded ankles and a silver flash down the sides. They must have cost a bomb.

"Yeah. Bought them in the States," she

was saying. "You can't get them over here."

"We're new to the neighbourhood," Mum said brightly.

"Oh, wow!" everyone said admiringly. Not to Mum, though.

"Arcacia Road," she went on, "just off the high street. Does anyone know it?"

"Brilliant!" everyone cooed.

Mum stretched out one arm and made a sudden little movement with her fingers towards my feet. I knew immediately what she was up to, but before I could step out of range it was too late. There was a slight sparking around my feet and for an instant it felt as if I'd stepped into icy water. When I looked down, I found I was wearing exactly the same trainers as the tall girl.

"Mum!" I said in anguish.

"Yes, quite a coincidence!" she said. "Look, everyone! Amber's got those trainers as well."

"Oh, wow!" Within a second they were all over me. "You've got them too! Fantastic!"

I gulped. "Yeah," I said faintly. "Good, aren't they?"

"Where did you get them?" the tall girl asked, frowning.

"They were a present," Mum said. "I had them flown over specially."

"Hmm," said the tall girl, giving me a funny look.

I smiled at her weakly.

"You didn't have them on earlier!" a chubby blonde girl said. "I passed you on the way to school and you weren't wearing them then."

I glowered at Mum. See! I wanted to say. This is how the trouble starts: someone *always* notices.

"She changed them!" Mum said quickly. "She changed them when she came into the playground."

The blonde girl eyed us. "Oh?" she said. Just like that. And I got the feeling that she already knew there was something odd about us.

Just then the bell went and everyone charged towards the two big doors at the front of the school, pushing and shoving to get inside first. Mum and I were right at the back, just behind the blonde girl, with roughly two hundred others in front of us.

"Witches don't like being last," Mum murmured, and then I felt her arm twitch. Before I could do anything to stop her, I had a blurred sensation of moving through the air at speed – and suddenly we were inside the school and the two hundred others were behind us.

Mum pulled me into an alcove as they rushed past on their way to their classrooms.

"What did you do that for?" I said crossly. "You promised you wouldn't draw attention to us."

"Witches don't like being at the back, darling. It doesn't suit our temperaments." She looked at me and shook her head rather sadly. "You should know that by now."

"Look, Mum," I said in a low, urgent voice. "You've done enough. You are *not* coming into the classroom with me."

She sighed. "How hurtful you are."

"I mean it, Mum. If you come in with me, I'm going to … to leave you and put myself up for adoption."

"You can't do that, darling. It's against the rules of the Witches' Charter."

"I don't care!" I said through gritted teeth. "You are *not* coming any further."

The chubby blonde girl who'd spoken to me earlier stopped beside us, frowning. "How did you get here so fast? I'm sure you were behind me in the playground."

Mum's eyes gleamed. "That's mag—"

"—magination!" I cut in swiftly.

"What?" the girl asked.

"Imagination," I said desperately. "You thought we were behind you, but we weren't."

"Yes, you were!" she said, puzzled.

There was a moment's awkward silence.

"Well anyway, here we both are now!" Mum said then, smiling sweetly at the girl. "Could you direct us to Mr Lemming's classroom, please?"

"Direct *me*," I said fiercely. "Me on my own."

"You're so hard on your poor mother," Mum sighed under her breath.

The girl nodded, still seeming puzzled. "Mr Lemming is my form teacher," she said.

"What luck," Mum said. "So you and Amber can be friends."

I glared at Mum, speechless with embarrassment and horror.

"I don't *think* so," the girl said.

NEIGHBOURHOOD

3

WITCH

"**E**xcuse my mum," I said, laughing nervously. "Mums, eh? How embarrassing can they get?"

"In your case, very embarrassing indeed," said the girl as we made our way along the corridor with a whole load of other girls.

We approached a flight of stone stairs. "Up here and right at the top," she pointed, tripping up as she spoke.

There weren't so many people about by then, and I felt brave enough to ask her name.

"Georgie," she said. "Short for Georgina."

"What's it like here?"

"It's OK," she said. "Pretty nice, really. Most of the girls are all right." She pulled a face. "With a few exceptions…"

"Who?" I asked.

"Well, Devlin, for a start," she said. "The girl with the trainers like yours." She glanced down at my feet as she spoke, and I did too, and then I gave a small gasp of horror and hoped she hadn't heard it. One of my trainers – luckily the one on the foot furthest away from her – had begun changing back into an ordinary shoe. All down one side the soft white and the silver flash had disappeared and there was now black leather and a heavy rubber sole.

To distract her I pointed at the paintings along the walls of the corridor. "They're great!" I said with pretend enthusiasm. "Are any of them yours?"

She shook her head, frowning. "No way! The first and second years did them."

Oops, I thought. "Well, they must be *very* advanced. So what's wrong with Devlin, then?" I asked quickly.

"Well, she's always having a go at me because..." Georgie began, and then she sighed. "You'll find out," she said.

At last we reached Mr Lemming's classroom. He was even older than my mum and a bit drippy-looking, with freckles and a blond moustache. He introduced me to the class, then pointed me towards a table at the back with five other girls. As I sat down, he asked if I'd prefer a seat by the window, but my right shoe was now turning back to normal so fast that I was frantic to shove my feet under the table and hide them. I shook my head and stayed where I was.

That afternoon, Georgie and I went into Art together. In spite of what she'd said earlier, she was really friendly. She had taken me into the dining hall at lunchtime and showed me where to queue up for food, and then we'd shared a table.

"Oh, you've changed into your ordinary shoes," she said as we sat down in the art room – unfortunately on Devlin's table, which was the only one with spaces.

They changed themselves, I felt like

saying. "Yes, I ... er ... didn't think those trainers were all that comfortable."

"*Mine* were made to measure," Devlin said immediately. "We had to pay extra but my dad said I was worth it." She looked at me. "I expect yours are the cheap version. Just copies."

"I shouldn't be surprised," I said. Mum's versions of things were *always* copies.

Devlin turned to Georgie with a mighty sigh. "D'you have to sit near me? Last week you spilt water everywhere – and the week before that you jogged me and ruined my drawing. You're so clumsy."

I'd already noticed that Georgie *was* clumsy. She seemed to be the sort who dropped things, fell over her own feet and bumped into people.

"I saw you in the queue at lunchtime,"

Devlin went on. "You tripped up and your sausages fell off your plate and rolled under the piano!"

Georgie went pink and didn't say anything, but three other girls sitting around Devlin sniggered.

And I decided I didn't like her.

In Art we had to make posters for the school fete, which was in three weeks' time. This fete was the school's Big Thing. It was how they got the money they needed for new books, theatre trips, plants for the gardens and all that. Mr Lemming had already talked to us long and rather boringly about it, and said that we must tell our families, friends and neighbours, who apparently were meant to come along and spend money buying stuff that they'd donated in the first place.

The posters we made were going to be put up all round the school grounds. We were given large sheets of charcoal-grey paper and told that as long as we included the right date and time, we could decorate them however we liked.

Georgie and I designed one together. I drew big, pencilled lettering and she filled in the letters with colour. Her brushwork was a bit blobby and she went over the edges of the letters. I didn't say anything though, because Devlin was working near us and making a great fuss every time Georgie moved: "Don't come near me, Georgie! Not an inch closer!" and "Aagghhh! Keep her away, everyone!"

At the end of the hour we were told to start clearing up, so I picked up a tub of blue poster paint and looked round for the lid. As I stood there, though – horrors! – Georgie jumped up and accidentally knocked into me, sending the tub flying and sploshing a fountain of bright blue paint all over Devlin's poster.

Devlin let out a bloodthirsty scream and advanced on Georgie as if she was about to strangle her. "You'll get it now, Georgina Mills!" she yelled. "Miss! Miss Garner! Georgie's ruined my poster! Miss…"

There was nothing else for it. Nothing at all. My arm started tingling and I knew I had to go for it.

"Wait!" I said. I happened to have a cloth over my arm and I rushed forward as if I was going to dab at the spoilt poster. What I actually did, though, was mutter a wish for the paint to disappear while extending my arm so that the magic could flow out of my fingertips.

It worked brilliantly. It worked like – well, like magic.

And I don't know who was more shocked – me, Georgie or Devlin.

NEIGHBOURHOOD
4
WITCH

"My little witchette! I'm so pleased!" Mum clucked when I told her what I'd done at school.

"Don't call me that!" I said grumpily. "And I'm *not* pleased."

"Your first spell." Mum smiled at me, tears welling in her eyes. "I've waited so long for this moment."

I groaned. "I didn't mean to do it. It just ... happened."

"That's the best way!" Mum said. "The very best. You did it instinctively. Without thinking. You're a witch whether you like it or not."

"I do not," I said very definitely. "And it's not going to happen again." I glanced at the table. "And you can put away the tall hat, the black cloak and that miniature broomstick. I don't want them!"

She smiled at me. A knowing smile. "All in good time, Amber."

I sighed. At school everyone had thought I'd somehow dabbed at the poster in just the right way and at just the right time, and cleaned off all the blue splodges. No one at all had suspected *magic*. Well, you wouldn't, would you?

"And just look at Mortimer," Mum went on. "He's beaming all over."

I looked at the cat. Its pouchy fat face was immobile, its eyes half-closed, its whiskers and ears downturned. "*Perlease*," I said. "It is *so* not beaming."

"You're thrilled, aren't you, Mortimer?" Mum cooed.

The cat flicked an ear towards us and then yawned, making a strange noise that was half meow and half growl.

"He said yes, he is, very thrilled indeed," Mum translated.

I looked at her suspiciously. I couldn't understand catspeak, though Mum said *she'd* been able to understand it since she was seven. It would come to me, apparently, when I was good and ready. Obviously not yet then...

"You were fantastic in Art!" Georgie said

on our way to school a couple of days later. And then she said, "Oops!" as she tripped up on the kerb. She bent to tie her shoelace. "I couldn't believe Devlin's face when she saw that you'd cleaned up all the paint and she couldn't attack me after all."

I nodded. "She was pretty gutted."

"I still don't know how you did it! When I try and clear up things, they always look worse."

I shrugged. "It was nothing," I said modestly, and as I spoke I felt that funny little tingle in my arm … a quiver reminding me that the magic was there, waiting for the next time I wanted to use it. Apparently, so Mum had told me, witches once had wands to make it easier to direct the magic to the right place, but things had evolved over the years and no one used them now. Anyway, it could tingle all it liked. *I was not going to use it again!*

We went through the school gates and walked over to the wall where everyone from our year seemed to congregate. Devlin was already there holding forth to her toadying friends, telling everyone which new CDs she had, which films she'd seen and which designer clothes she'd bought. Then she got on to a new subject.

"I'm going to ask my cousin to come to the fete," Devlin said. "His name's Snap Snaker and he's a DJ on local radio." She looked round to make sure everyone was listening. "He's in with all the stars. I'm going to ask him to bring someone *very famous* along with him."

Some people looked impressed. Georgie and I didn't.

There was a pause, then a girl called Hazel said, "I'm going to bring my horse in and give rides up and down the field for fifty pence a time."

Devlin turned her nose up. "Horses stink! Isn't anyone doing anything decent?"

"My mum's going to make chocolate brownies," said Georgie.

"Yuck!" Devlin said and pulled a face. "I wouldn't want to eat anything coming from your house. If your mum's like you, she'll get the recipe muddled up and drop the mixture on the floor."

"No, she won't," Georgie said, frowning. "My mum makes really ace brownies."

"Well, Snap Snaker is *brilliant*. He knows everyone: bands, footballers … the prime minister! He gets all the soap stars on his show."

"*All* of them?" I asked.

"Yes!"

"Well, if he gets a few of them to come to the fete, they could sell their autographs and earn us lots of money," a girl called Sasha said.

"He'll ask them all right!" Devlin boasted. "He'll do anything for me!"

Her smarmy friends made noises of praise and appreciation.

"So, what else are you doing for the fete?" she asked Georgie in a withering tone. "Falling on your face and giving everyone a laugh?"

Georgie didn't say anything.

"Bet *you* don't know anyone famous!"

"Yes, I do," Georgie said suddenly. "I know Daniel Stanley and I've asked him to come and open the fete."

There was a stunned silence and then everyone gasped or said, "Wow!" because however many prime ministers Devlin's cousin knew (if he knew any), this was nothing to someone actually knowing Daniel Stanley. He was the fittest, cleverest, most highly paid footballer in the world, and he was married to a supermodel. He had rippling muscles and dark curls, and everyone was mad about him.

"You haven't! Wicked!" everyone said, and they gathered round Georgie as if a little bit of Daniel Stanley might be clinging to her.

"*What?*" Devlin said, looking both horrified and outraged.

"You heard me," said Georgie carelessly.

"Why didn't you tell us before?" Hazel asked.

"I've … er … been saving it up to surprise you."

"And he's really going to open our fete?" Sasha asked, mouth gaping.

"That's right."

"How d'you know him?" someone else wanted to know.

"Oh, he's a friend of my big brother," said Georgie carelessly.

The bell went then, and after a few more rounds of *"Wow!"* *"Top!"* and *"Fantastic!"* everyone started moving off towards the doors.

I sighed. "Daniel Stanley is totally brilliant," I said to Georgie. "I can't wait to see him."

She looked at me from the corner of her eye. "You might have a long wait."

"What d'you mean?"

"I made it up!" she whispered. "I wanted to do something to get back at Devlin and it came out before I could stop it."

I gaped at her. "But you've told *everyone* now."

"I know." She looked at me hopelessly. "What am I going to do? I'll have to run away."

My arm started twitching and my fingers felt as if they had pins and needles shooting from them. I knew what was going on – *something* was trying to say that this was a good opportunity to try a bit of magic. I didn't know what I could do, though – and I wasn't going to try.

I was *so* not going to try…

NEIGHBOURHOOD
5
WiTCH

In Art we were working on our posters again. They should have been up outside the school by now, attracting the attention of passers-by, but Miss Garner said they needed to be smartened up and given more *oomph*.

"I want you all to concentrate on the day itself," she said. "What do you think is the main attraction? What will bring in the crowds? What is it that will make people get up out of their armchairs and come along to our fete?"

No one replied; we were all too busy thinking.

"When you've decided what that important thing is – and I want lots of different ideas – add it to your poster!"

"I think it's competitions and big prizes!" Sasha said after a moment.

"Home-made cakes," someone else said.

"A white-elephant stall," Marie suggested. "My mum always likes those best."

Devlin shook her head. "No, it's none of those!" she said. "What people want is to meet someone famous. And the someone they'll all want to meet is Snap Snaker the DJ and his friends!"

Georgie pretended to be busy studying our poster. We'd decided that if we didn't say another word about Daniel Stanley, tried to forget he'd ever been mentioned, then Devlin might...

As if.

"Still, my Snap is going to be overshadowed, isn't he?" she said to Georgie, "Because your friend... He *is* your friend, isn't he?"

Georgie went pink. "My brother's friend..." she mumbled.

"Your brother's friend, Daniel Stanley, is actually coming along to open our fete! *Probably*."

Her toadies squealed with laughter.

"Have you heard, Miss Garner?" Devlin called. "Georgie has invited Daniel Stanley!"

Miss Garner smiled. "Daniel Stanley! We wish, eh, girls?"

"No, really," Devlin said. "Daniel Stanley *is* coming. Tell her, Georgie."

Georgie smiled weakly. "Yes, he is," she said in a whisper.

"Speak up!" Devlin said. "Tell Miss Garner all about it."

"I've … er … asked Daniel Stanley to open the fete," Georgie said.

Miss Garner laughed. "Yes, and William Shakespeare too, I shouldn't wonder. Who is it, Georgie, someone who looks like him?"

"No, he's the real thing," Devlin answered for her. "I mean, I thought it was exciting having my cousin coming, but now I know Daniel Stanley will be there, it's hardly worth him getting out of bed. I'd better get him along, though…" and here she gave Georgie a devious look, "just in case Daniel Stanley doesn't turn up."

"*Ha ha!*" shrieked the toadies.

Georgie gulped. "Well, it *is* possible that he'll be playing in an important cup final that day."

"In September?" Devlin said. "I don't think so. Don't you know anything about football?" She smiled cruelly. "I tell you what, Georgie, Daniel Stanley is so special that we should put his name on every poster." She leaned right back in her chair so she could see across the room. "Everyone!" she commanded. "Put on your posters that Daniel Stanley..."

I shot a quick look at Georgie. She was turning red instead of pink and – well, I couldn't just *sit* there, could I? I straightened my left arm, as if I was stretching it, and sent a little shiver of magic towards

Devlin. Her chair gently tipped over and with a squeal of astonishment she landed on her back on the floor.

As a toady rushed to pick her up, Miss Garner asked, "Are you all right, Devlin? I'm always telling you girls not to go back on your chairs like that. See what can happen?"

Devlin got to her feet, glowering, and Miss Garner added, "And that's quite enough about Daniel Stanley. The rest of you get on with your *own* ideas for your posters now, please!"

I blinked, and then quickly put my left arm behind my back, as if I was trying to hide something incriminating. The magic had almost worked on its own that time. A bit worrying, that...

6

NEIGHBOURHOOD WITCH

"It's really nice that you've come to tea," Mum said as Georgie and I went into the kitchen. "I just knew that you and Amber would be friends."

I shot Mum a glance. I was never sure whether things like that – becoming friends with people – were due to me and the person just happening to get along or to Mum's interference and a spell. Best not to ask, I thought.

Georgie pulled out a chair to sit down and found Mortimer there, slobbed out like a great furry cushion.

"Oh, just ask him to get off," Mum said. "No, on second thoughts, *you'd* better ask him, Amber. In case he turns funny."

"Off you get, Mortimer!" I said, in the bright sort of voice ordinary people use to talk to their ordinary cats.

"Amber!" Mum said. "Nicely, please."

I didn't dare look at Georgie. "Please, Mortimer, can my friend sit on that chair?" I said in a syrupy voice. "If it's all right with you, that is…"

Georgie laughed, as if going along with the joke, but Mortimer gave me a one-eyed frown. Thankfully, though, he must have been in a good mood because he slipped down the other side of the chair, making a deep growly noise.

"There, he said he didn't mind a bit," said Mum. Georgie laughed again, brushed off the fur and sat down.

"I'm going to make some sandwiches with my home-made bread," Mum said.

Georgie nodded. "That'd be lovely. Thanks."

"And for filling you can either have bat's wing, eye of newt or lark's tongue with mayonnaise."

Georgie looked startled, and I looked daggers at Mum. As I said, she does like to fly her broomstick close to the wind.

"Sorry, Georgie," I said. "My mum thinks she's being funny. Cheese or egg?"

"Oh, egg, please." Georgie glanced round the room. "What an unusual room. It's very … er … cosy and different."

I looked at her anxiously. Before she'd arrived, I'd made Mum hide the ornamental cauldron, our big glass seeing-ball, the bunches of dried herbs and grasses and the dangling crystals at the windows. Mum said I was being silly and that you could get away with stuff like that – that it just looked New Agey – but I didn't want to take any chances. On the window we had a sign saying:

Herbal potions – come and try!

but I thought that was OK, seeing as everyone was doing herbal remedies these days.

"In what way ... different?" I asked as Mum washed salad at the sink. Under her breath she was singing:

*"A witch is a treasure,
a wonderful thing..."*

"Well," said Georgie. "As I said, it's very cosy. And … dark."

This darkness business was something I hadn't been able to do anything about. Neighbourhood Witches' houses are decorated by the WI so no matter where you're posted, your furnishings are the same: dark-blue walls to look like the night sky and black curtains, black sofas and black just-about-everything-else. Witches are very fond of black. *Black is the new black*, as Mum is keen on saying.

She put our sandwiches on the table. "Now," she said, "what would you like to drink? Bat's blood all right for you, Georgie?"

Georgie burst into laughter. "Your mum's really funny."

"Mmm…" I said grimly.

But she sometimes takes a joke too far.

All went well after that, until we went into the sitting-room to watch TV. There wasn't much on and Mum was zapping between channels hoping to find a re-run of *Buffy* when Georgie said in a startled voice, "How d'you do that, Mrs Collins?"

I looked at Mum, alarmed. I hadn't seen her doing anything odd. What hadn't I noticed?

"Do what, dear?" Mum asked.

"How do you change channels without using a remote control?" Georgie asked. "I've been watching – you just pointing your fingers at the set."

"Ah…" Mum said.

I froze while I tried to think of an explanation. Mum had used magic to zap across the channels ever since Mortimer rolled on our remote control and broke it. She'd been doing it for ages and I'd got used to it.

"It's…" Mum began.

"It's just that some people have electricity in their body!" I burst out.

Georgie frowned. "I don't understand," she said.

"It's like – you know, sometimes you get an electric shock from metal rails and things?" I improvised madly. "Well, Mum has extra electricity in her body – so much that she can change the TV channels!"

"Wow!" Georgie said, wide-eyed. "That's amazing. You ought to go on stage or something. Is there anything else you can do?"

"Oh, yes!" Mum said, only too ready to tell her. "I can move…"

"Radio stations as well!" I exclaimed. And then I practically pulled Georgie from the room, reminding her that we had important things to discuss upstairs.

In my bedroom, the door tightly closed against listeners, we talked about Devlin and what we were going to do about the fete.

"If only I hadn't said anything about Daniel Stanley," Georgie sighed. "She's never going to let me forget it!"

I shook my head. "She's getting worse and worse," I said. For the last few days Devlin had been unbearable, never missing a chance to be nasty to Georgie, to goad and bully her.

"What about writing to him – to Daniel Stanley?" I said. "Maybe if we told him exactly what happened, he'd take pity on us."

Georgie shook her head miserably. "I wrote to him last year to ask for his autograph and he didn't even reply."

I wasn't surprised. He might have been gorgeous, but Daniel Stanley had a reputation for keeping himself to himself since he'd become an international star. When he wasn't playing football or making personal appearances, he just stayed in his country house and kept away from people.

"Well, what about this: on the day of the fete we could send a message and pretend it's come from him, saying that he's been unavoidably delayed?" I said.

"Huh!" Georgie said. "Everyone would see through that straight away."

I nodded gloomily. "You're right."

We went on like this for the rest of the evening, with first me and then Georgie thinking of some pathetic way out that wasn't a real way out at all, and then suddenly it was seven-thirty and Georgie's mum was knocking on the door.

When she'd gone I went into the kitchen to snaffle a couple of biscuits. Mum was there, standing at the kitchen table and pounding herbs in a pestle and mortar. A line of newly filled jars and medicine bottles stood along a shelf. "Have you been down here all this time?" I asked her. I hadn't said much to her about the fete, because this was just the sort of thing that a neighbourhood witch was supposed to get involved with. And I was determined that a certain neighbourhood witch I knew was *not*.

She nodded. "I've been very busy making lotions and potions and herbal concoctions, so you needn't think I've been hanging about outside your door listening to you."

"No?"

"Certainly not. I sent Mortimer instead!" she cackled. "Now, who is this Daniel Stanley and why d'you want him to come to your fete?"

NEIGHBOURHOOD
7
WiTCH

It was Saturday, and Mum was feeling very pleased with herself because she'd just given an old neighbour some healing balm for a painful bunion, and stopped someone else's continuous sneezing by burning herbs and making them sniff the ashes.

"Good traditional remedies," she said to me with satisfaction afterwards. "None of your factory-made chemicals for us neighbourhood witches!" She glanced over to where I was sitting at the kitchen table, working on some homework. "Never mind all that school stuff – you'd be far better off learning about herbs and cures from me."

"I *have* to do school stuff," I said. "We've got tests soon."

"Tests! Hocus-pocus!" she said. "You don't have to worry about tests. You've already got a job waiting for you when you leave school."

Mortimer growled from the next chair.

"And a cat, too, of course."

"Yeah. Wonderful," I said. (It was OK saying things like that, because Mortimer didn't understand sarcasm.)

"Just think, darling. You'll work as my assistant until I park my broomstick, and then take on a community of your very own."

I sighed. "Will I *have* to?"

"Of course," she said, filling the last bottle.

I pushed my books to one side. "Didn't you ever want to do something else though, Mum? Something different?"

"Never!" she said stoutly. "I knew my destiny. Always remember,

A neighbourhood witch
is a wonderful..."

"I know, I know!" I said hastily. "But years ago, when you were my age, didn't you want to do something *different*?"

She reached for her manicure set, sat down and began to buff her fingernails. Neighbourhood witches, the same as all other witches, love having long and shapely fingernails. Some of them even open nail salons. "I think … maybe … right at the beginning, I might have wanted to try something else," she said. "But I came round, darling. And you will, too! It's your heritage."

"Hmm," I said, and wished, not for the first time, that we knew other neighbourhood witches so I could speak to their daughters and find out how they felt about the whole witch business.

She buffed and filed and varnished (black enamel, of course), then took some little shiny crescent moons and stuck one on the tip of each nail. They looked a bit common, actually, but she wouldn't be told.

I went back to my homework and she picked up the local paper and began going through it with a felt-tip pen, circling the notices for lost cats and dogs, jotting down details of anyone who might need some shopping done, or noting an address where someone had come out of hospital and could do with a herbal tonic. These people would have a visit from a strange woman with long, black fingernails who "just happened to be passing".

"There's a full-page advertisement for your fete here. Does everyone go?"

I nodded. "Everyone and their auntie is supposed to turn out."

"Is there a fancy-dress competition?"

"Only for under-tens," I said.

"Pity!" she said. "I would have gone as—"

"Yes, Mum," I interrupted. "I think I can work that one out."

She turned to the next page and suddenly exclaimed, "Daniel Stanley!"

"What about him?"

She read:

> The country's top footballer, Daniel Stanley, and his lovely wife, Gloria, will open the vast new sports complex, Stanley Stadium, in Burnham next Saturday morning. They will arrive by helicopter and then tour the streets by car. Very large crowds are expected and police are being drafted in from the three neighbouring forces to keep them under control.

"Next Saturday!" I said. The day of the fete. And the day that Georgie was going to have to admit that she'd made the whole Daniel Stanley thing up...

"So he's going to be nearby," Mum said. Her eyes gleamed and looked just like Mortimer's.

"No!" I said. "Before you even say it – *no*."

"I was just going to suggest a little trip to the new stadium," she said innocently. "You, me and Georgie…"

"No!" I said again. I would have loved even a glimpse of Daniel Stanley, but I didn't want Mum to start doing magic all over the place.

"It'll be the only chance you'll get…" she wheedled.

I frowned. "Look, I wouldn't mind going to see him – and maybe, if we got half a chance, asking him to come to the fete. But you needn't think you'll be able to talk me into doing any magic on him."

She flapped her hand dismissively. "You wouldn't be able to do big magic like that, darling. I doubt if I could, even. Anything which involves stars and celebrities doesn't come within a neighbourhood witch's powers; it would be in *superwitch* league."

"Hmm…" I said. In my experience, knowing Mum couldn't do something never stopped her from having a go – and usually making a complete hash of it. This time I didn't want her to try. I liked living where we were, I liked school and I liked Georgie – and I didn't want anyone to start thinking there was something funny about us. "No," I said firmly. "You're not going!"

"Just as you like, darling."

"And neither am I."

My fingers were crossed, of course.

NEIGHBOURHOOD
8
WiTCH

"This looks like a good place to stand," Georgie said on Saturday, after we'd struggled through the crowds in town. "When he comes out of the stadium, his car will have to slow down on this corner and he's bound to see us."

I nodded. "I'll get the banner out."

We'd made a long paper banner and we'd wave it like mad.

It said:

It was worth a try, we thought. Better than nothing.

Mum was well out of the way. She'd been invited to a meeting – a proper neighbourhood watch meeting ("watch" with an "a") – where she was going to be introduced to everyone in our road. She'd have a whole new set of people to be nosy about and with luck wouldn't even think about what I was up to.

"OK, I'll hold this end," I said, unrolling the banner carefully. "And you hold the other."

"D'you think it'll work?" Georgie asked,

to our fete!
Burnham. Two o'Clock!

nibbling her bottom lip.

"Don't know," I said. "If it doesn't—"

"If it doesn't, my life won't be worth living."

Devlin had really had it in for Georgie these last couple of days, following her about and holding loud, imaginary conversations along the lines of, *"Oooh, Daniel Stanley, it's so wonderful that you've come to our fete."* After the fete had actually happened and he actually *hadn't* turned up, she was going to be totally unbearable.

So this was our last hope...

* * *

Two hours later the helicopter bringing Daniel and Gloria had landed in the stadium, and the crowds of people waiting for them to drive past were five or six deep. By lashing our jumpers around ourselves and tying them to the railings, though, we'd managed to stay in front with our banner.

He just had to see it…

A rumour had spread through the crowd that Daniel was leaving the stadium and would be coming past soon, and a few moments after that we heard the rumble of an extended cheer further down the high street.

Then disaster struck.

Georgie, forgetting that she was holding one end of our banner, waved her arms in excitement, then lost her balance. She grabbed the railings for support and in doing so managed to tear the long strip of paper in half. It immediately fell to the ground and got trodden on by the crowds pushing forward behind us.

Georgie looked at me in anguish. "Sorry!" she said. "I just slipped…"

I looked back at her bleakly. My fingers started tingling and I knew I could probably have worked some magic to get the banner up and mended, but Georgie was standing much too close and I'd never have been able to explain it. Besides, I reminded myself again, I didn't *want* to do magic.

"Oh, well," I said. "We'll just have to shout."

"And then go on to the fete and face Devlin…" Georgie said despondently.

A moment later the car came into sight and everyone around us began waving and shouting, pushing to get to the front and see the famous pair.

Two motorcycle outriders came down the street first, followed by a red, open-topped limo driven by a chauffeur. In the second row of seats there they were: Daniel Stanley and Gloria. In person.

"Daniel!" we screamed. *"Gloria!"*

"We love you!" someone behind us yelled.

I nudged Georgie. "Ready?"

She nodded. "One, two, three," we counted together. Then, "Come – to – our – fete!" we roared at the top of our voices as the car drove past.

But although we were yelling as loudly as we could, our voices were lost in all the clamour and Daniel never even turned his head.

"Oh no!" I wailed, "it's hopeless!" And Georgie just gave a cry of distress.

There was a sudden down-draft of cold air. "Anything I can do?" a voice asked in my ear.

"Mum!"

"Mrs Collins!" Georgie said in surprise. "How did you get here?"

"By WATER," Mum said, meaning Witches Alternative Transport. "So efficient."

"I didn't know that the river—" Georgie began.

"She's just joking," I said hurriedly. I frowned at Mum. "You've missed him."

"Oh, I don't think so," said Mum. "Not entirely." And as the red car drew away from us she stretched out one arm, as if she was waving, and then closed her eyes tightly. This went unnoticed while everyone else was watching the car go on its way.

"Help me, darling!" Mum said to me in a low voice. "We've got one chance to get him back."

I thought fast; weighing things up. On the one hand embarrassment and scorn, on the other...

Well, what's a girl to do?

I put out my arm close to Mum's, and the magic streamed down it in a tingly-pins-and-needles wave of feeling and reached towards Daniel Stanley.

And suddenly the car wasn't going on its way at all.

"They're coming back!" someone screeched, and to everyone's amazement the red car went into reverse and came slowly back ... and back ... until it stopped right in front of where we were standing. Daniel Stanley sat there, looking at us, bemused. And Gloria looked as if she'd been hit with a wet herring.

Mum dropped her arm. "Phew! I wasn't sure we could do that," she said. "It took it out of me, I can tell you." She nudged me. "Speak up, then! Say what you want to say."

I swallowed hard, and then called over, "Daniel and Gloria – will you come and open our school fete this afternoon?"

"Please, please, please!" added Georgie all in a panic and a flurry.

Daniel's mouth opened and closed, and he shook his head slightly. It looked as if he was trying to say "Sorry" and "No", but the sounds didn't come out like that. Instead everyone around us heard him, very distinctly, say, "Yes. Jump in the back."

Georgie and I looked at each other.

And then we jumped.

As the car moved off again we sat there sliding about on the soft leather seat. Georgie looked at me with such total amazement that I couldn't help but burst out laughing.

"Where to?" came the message from the chauffeur. We told him, then heard it repeated in the crowd. As we drove off Mum was telling everyone around her, "Yes, that's right. Cheetham School. Two o'clock!"

We were early so we took the long way round (Daniel and Gloria weren't nearly so stand-offish as we'd heard, and actually liked waving to people) and the chauffeur phoned the Head and the police to say we were coming. As we approached our school just before two o'clock, Georgie and I were practically gibbering with excitement – especially as there was not only a big crowd waiting, but also a TV broadcast van.

We drove through the school gates waving to everyone as if *we* were the celebrities. It was then that the best thing of all happened – the limo went through a puddle, and water whooshed up and splashed a girl who was standing there staring at us in amazement. And that girl was Devlin!

After we'd stopped laughing, Georgie turned to me. "This is so brilliant, I can't believe it!" she said. "I reckon your mum must be a witch."

Completely taken aback, I looked at her in horror. "*What?*" I said. "Of course she's not. How could you say such a thing? She's just an ordinary mum. She hasn't got a cauldron or a witch's hat or…"

Georgie beamed at me. "I was only joking!" she said. "I was just thinking how great it was that once your mum suddenly turned up like that, everything started to go right. It was like – well, it was like magic."

I swallowed hard "These things happen," I said.

Well, they did with a mum like mine.

ABOUT THE AUTHOR

Mary Hooper knows more than most people what makes a good story – she's had over six hundred published in teenage and women's magazines, such as *J17*, and is the highly regarded author of over fifty titles for young people, including *Best Friends, Worst Luck*; *The Great Twin Trick*; *Mad About the Boy*; *The Boyfriend Trap*; the "Spook" books and the Letters to Liz series. She recently won the North East Book Award for her teenage novel *Megan*. Mary has two grown-up children, Rowan and Gemma, and lives in an old cottage in Hampshire.

BEST FRIENDS, WORST LUCK
Mary Hooper

Moving from the city to a new life in the country is not Bev's idea of fun. Who will she find to talk to? What will she find to do? And how on earth will she manage without her best friend Sal?

"Sharp-witted… Great fun."
The Daily Telegraph